Baby For The Alphan Captain

Alien Baby Pact, Volume 4

Aurelia Skye and Juno Wells

Published by Amourisa Press, 2023.

JOIN JUNO WELLS' NEW RELEASE LIST!

Click on this link (or copy and paste it into your browser): http://eepurl.com/bnMJL5

Cover Images: Depositphotos.com

Cover Design: Amourisa Press

Join Kit's Mailing List[1] **(www.kittunstall.com/newsletter) to receive notification of new releases and access bonus chapters for your favorite books. You get free books just for signing up. If you prefer to receive notifications for just one, or a few, of Kit's pen names, you'll have the option to select which lists to subscribe to at signup.**

---

1. http://kittunstall.com/newsletter/

Blurb

A runaway proxy, a determined Alphan, and a searing claim that marks them both.

FIVE MONTHS AGO, PEI Ling Xiang's life was turned upside down when Earth authorities broke into the bunker where her family had sheltered for the last eleven years, dragging her parents to prison and taking her and her sister to the Faction Embassy to be registered as proxies. When she learned she would be paired with an Alphan, she panicked and fled. If Brighton hadn't taken her in, she would have been in a desperate situation. Once he catches her, she settles in with Zafer and grows to care for him, but her family is still at risk.

Zafer Karr spent five months tracking his wayward proxy, and once he acquires her, he tasks himself with winning her trust and proving she's safe with him. He believes he's succeeded, and she weathers her first omegan heat without fear, so he's mystified when she disappears again. He won't let her go without a fight, because he loves his stubborn human and wants to make her his mate forever, not just a year.

Seven years ago, the Faction agreed to save Earth from the Vorathan invasion in exchange for Earth women giving them one year of proxy rights to act as a surrogate, since the aliens of the Faction faced a dwindling population. With the Vorathans feared throughout the galaxy as bloodthirsty, vicious marauders, the Earth's government agreed.

That doesn't mean the women did.

Sometimes, you want to read about the entire alien empire and all its myriad twists and turns, immersing yourself in hundreds of pages of intrigue. And sometimes, you want to skip the frills and get to the main event. Juno and Aurelia are pleased to bring you a series of short, steamy romances about untouched human women making babies with their truly alien mates.

Prologue

Pei Ling

PEI LING XIANG AND her family had been lucky. They'd spent most of the invasion living in an exclusive bunker in what had once been Wyoming. Her father had moved them from Singapore to the locale when the vorathans first invaded. She'd had a positively idyllic childhood and young adulthood compared to anyone living on the surface, but the discovery of the bunker ripped it all away.

In one night, the newly unified Earth government had drilled into their home and sent in troops to collect all the women who were supposed to be registered for the draft. Pei Ling had been one of them, having avoided the fate until then. At twenty-one, she'd assumed she would live in the bunker for the rest of her life. Instead, she'd been virtually arrested, though the Earth forces assured her it was her parents who would face legal actions, not her, as long as she went along with her obligations.

She'd tried. Pei Ling had been taken to the Faction Embassy for testing. Within hours, they'd told her she was best suited to match with alphans. Hours after that, they'd placed her before a vidscreen to meet the alphan captain who planned to claim her for his proxy right.

Recalling it even now made her tremble both with a touch of desire and a surge of fear. His blue countenance had been oddly striking, with his short navy-blue hair, large blue eyes, and broad, sculpted features. His muscled physique had intrigued her. Living in the bunker, there hadn't been many options for dating. Most of the people were younger or older than her, or they were her siblings. The first flicker of curiosity and desire for the alien had surprised her.

His voice had been deep and rough, but somehow pleasing. "You are a beautiful human," he'd said in that raspy tone.

It had sent shivers down her spine. Pei Ling had tried to respond with a smile and kind words, but she'd only managed a shy, "Thank you." She hadn't confessed her own interest in him because it felt too bold, and she was afraid.

"My shift ends in a few Earth hours, and I can teleport down to meet you. I'm serving an Earth rotation for the rest of this year and part of next. After that, we...I will travel to Baxa."

She'd nodded at the information.

He had sighed. Zafer Karr clearly expected more conversation from her. "We'll discuss more when I arrive."

"Yes, Captain Karr," she'd said quietly.

"Call me Zafer, Pei Ling." At her nod, he'd sighed again and ended the vidcall.

The proctor, a human man in a long black coat styled after the Faction's dress uniforms, had returned then. "The captain will be here in a few hours. In the meantime, there's much you should learn about the alphan mating process. After you've had a chance to study this material, I'll take you for your genetic modification."

She'd swallowed. "My what?"

He frowned. "It's a simple injection, Ms. Xiang. It modifies your reproductive system and uterus to be able to carry an alphan offspring. There's some hormonal modification involved as well, to induce an omegan heat cycle."

Pei Ling had stared at him in confusion. "A...what?"

He'd looked at his wrist comm in an impatient way. "I don't have time to explain what's on the datapad. Read it and prepare yourself."

After he walked out, Pei Ling had reluctantly started reading. She'd read for nearly an hour, and her fear had grown with each word she read. By the time she scrolled to the end, she'd had enough information to be terrified about the process, but not enough to truly understand it. It sounded like the modification turned her into his helpless broodmare, ready any time he wanted to claim her. She might have to endure that for a year, but she couldn't allow herself to be changed to like that, could she?

In a fit of panic, she'd run from the Embassy. The consequences hadn't seemed nearly as dire as submitting to the legal obligations enacted on her behalf by the various governments of Earth when the Faction presented their demands in exchange for protection. There was no way the situation could have been bad enough that they felt it was okay to trade the rights and autonomy of a woman for an entire year or more of reproductive and sexual servitude to alien species.

She'd spent a few days roughing it on the streets, distraught to see how much Earth differed from the images she'd seen in her education, which had focused mostly on pre-invasion aspects. She'd questioned her conclusion that there was no reason for Earth to trade their women for protection a few times, but she couldn't bring herself to return to the Embassy.

Then Brighton had found her. She'd spent three months living with the other woman before Brighton was summoned to be the surrogate for a Brundle commander. After that, Pei Ling had been alone the last two months. She wasn't very good at being alone, but it seemed preferable to surrendering to modification to make her an omegan.

The last few days had been different. She had stopped leaving the POD at all, convinced someone was watching her. Her senses were heightened, and she was running continuously on adrenaline. She hated this feeling and almost considered turning herself into the Embassy. The alphan captain had probably claimed a different human by now, but five years in an Earth prison seemed preferable to the vulnerability of living alone in this rough neighborhood.

And what would she do when the nutrients in the synthicator ran out, and it wasn't refilled, since the POD wasn't registered as a dwelling for anyone now? That was still three to four months away, but she was already frightened. She'd never missed a meal until that terrifying time she'd been on the streets after running, and she didn't want to go back to that aching hunger in her belly.

All that still wasn't enough to make her want to surrender to the Embassy, but with someone watching her, she was afraid it might be one of the street gangs who prowled the neighborhoods. They struck the most vulnerable, targeting them for crimes of all sorts. Brighton had warned her, and they'd never ventured out after nightfall.

That was all going through her head as she heard the POD alarms trip that night. Silver moonlight shone through the sunroof in her room, and she reached over to press a button to add the privacy shading. Her heart trembled as she got out of bed and quickly dressed in a simple white jumpsuit she'd found in Brighton's things, left behind by one of her former roommates. It was a one-piece but not nearly as pretty or fashionable as the one she'd worn when the government burst into the bunker and uprooted her life, along with everyone else who'd lived there.

She had no intention of going outside, but her heart skipped a beat and she let out a small cry of shock when the main door made a chiming sound right before it opened. She looked for a place to hide, but there was nowhere. Her heart was in her throat as she squeezed into the closet and hoped whoever was breaking in didn't know the POD was inhabited. With luck, they were there to scavenge and wouldn't look too closely for her.

Her hopes fled when the door opened a few moments later. She didn't get much of a glance at who stood before her. It appeared to be a tall male, and as her eyes adjusted to the light from the room filtering into the black closet, she recognized blue skin. "Zafer?" she asked in a quiet voice filled with dread but perhaps a small trace of secret longing.

His impatient sigh was all too familiar, but he didn't speak. Instead, he shot a spray of red gas in her face. It made her giddy, and she collapsed forward, unaware of anything beyond that point.

Chapter One

FINALLY, HE'D TRACKED the human woman to this slum. It hadn't been easy to find Pei Ling Xiang, his assigned proxy, but he'd been diligent, devoting every spare moment he had to finding her after she'd fled from the Faction Embassy after they'd spoken five months ago. He'd been coming to her via teleporting from the Spaceport in orbit above Earth once his shift ended. By the time he'd arrived, she'd panicked and fled.

To his annoyance, she'd fled before modification and tagging, so he'd had a rough time finding her. The Faction had lent assistance, but they were spread thin, as were Earth authorities. It had taken him a while to cultivate the right contacts around the city, but he'd finally found a gang willing to spy for him. They'd watched her for a few days and assured him it was his proxy.

He'd been pleasantly surprised to find they were right. Not taking any chances, he immediately gassed her to sleep and opened the door completely. He picked up Pei Ling and slung her over his shoulder, grunting in surprise. She was considerably lighter than he'd expected, and he worried she was malnourished.

He was irritated at the time he'd lost, and the effort he'd undertaken to secure her, but he was also concerned about her.

She had to be in good health to bear him a child, and he very much wanted to be a father.

"I've had no family for a long time, Pei Ling," he said to her unconscious form as he strode from the POD. A few of the gang members waited nearby, and he gave them the agreed-upon rathium bar.

"The POD is empty?" asked one of the girls, who had a lean face and a look of prolonged hunger. She didn't seem old enough for the draft.

He nodded. "You can probably get a few rathium chips for the contents."

The girl's eyes widened as her belly rumbled. "I'm more interested in the synthicator nutrient levels." She rushed toward it.

The other four gang members followed behind her, and he headed to his skid. He'd borrowed it from the Embassy after teleporting from the spaceport, since it was the easiest way to travel when one was on Earth rotation.

Now, he used it to return to the Embassy. As they reached the skid parking, he stopped and hopped down, noticing she was waking. She stirred over his shoulder, so he tightened his hold. She started to kick and squirm a moment later. "Let me down."

His teeth gritted at the shrill sound. alphans had sensitive hearing, and it irked him. "Lower your tone."

That only incensed her, and she got shriller, making more incoherent demands as he strode into the Embassy. He was amused at the way others gave them a wide berth as he took her straight to Medbay, ignoring a proctor who tagged along.

"Have you found her, Captain?" asked the young man in the black coat.

He grunted and kept going, not stopping until they'd reached Medbay. Then he dropped her on an exam table and pinned her in to keep her from running as Med Chief Quillin approached. The golden mosaic alien was a combination of various aliens stitched together to keep their race alive. If not for the mosaics, they wouldn't know how to alter human DNA to make a woman fertile with an alien but not significantly change her own DNA.

"This is Pei Ling Xiang?" asked Quillin.

"Let me out of here," said Pei Ling, still trying to get past Zafer.

He put a hand on her shoulder, lightly squeezing, but not to hurt her. "Calm yourself, human."

She glared at him. "I don't want to calm myself, alphan. I want out of here."

The proctor stepped forward with a severe expression. "You're lucky Captain Karr was willing to search for you, Ms. Xiang. If he hadn't overlooked your defiance, you'd be in prison now. If you refuse to do your civic duty, you'll automatically receive five years in a federal facility. There's nothing your family's money can do to buy you out of this." His voice dripped with disdain.

Zafer, feeling oddly protective, turned to the proctor. He flashed his fangs when he growled. "Out."

"But, sir—"

"We'll handle this ourselves. Threatening her isn't going to conquer her fear, proctor." He growled the words.

The young man's eyes widened, and he scurried from Medbay.

Quillin laughed. "As diplomatic as ever, Zafer."

Zafer grinned before turning his attention to Pei Ling. "I mean you no harm, human woman. I want a child, and your government agreed to this situation. I understand your fears, but you won't be harmed."

"No, I'll just be expected to give you a child and walk away after you turn me into some sort of submissive sex slave."

He frowned. "I...what?"

"She's referring to being modified to have an omegan receptor. It's a necessary part of the modification." Quillin's voice softened when he turned to Pei Ling. "It isn't how you imagine. The procedure will trigger a natural heat. During that time, your alphan mate will be irresistible, and you will spend much of your time mating. After the heat ends, you'll return to a normal level of intimacy...or not, depending on the couple. You're likely to be pregnant following your first heat."

She didn't look any less frightened. Zafer felt bad for her, but it couldn't be helped. "I'll be there to guide you."

She looked skeptical, and her deep brown eyes welled with tears, but she blinked them back after a moment. "Fine. What choice do I have, right? It's a one-year sentence or a five-year sentence." She sniffled, looking a tad pathetic.

He brushed a furred knuckle down her cheek, making her shiver. He didn't think it was in displeasure from the way her eyes widened, and he sensed a shift in her pheromones. The modification would only increase his ability to detect her pheromones, and he was eager to experience it as her mate. Not mate, he scolded himself. He couldn't count on this becoming permanent.

Quillin had been preparing the injection while she spoke, and now he used the hypodermic to put it in via her upper arm.

"You might have some side effects for a few hours, but mostly, you'll probably just want to sleep." He looked at Zafer. "You can take her to your ship now and let her rest for a while."

Zafer nodded, stepping forward to pick her up.

"I can walk," she said with a hint of shrillness.

"I'd rather not risk it." He didn't want to spend another five months chasing her, though with her being tagged now, she'd be much easier to track. It didn't sit well with him to have to tag and track her, so he'd rather ensure she came with him as willingly as possible.

She tried to squirm away as he strode through the Embassy to the teleport station. When he'd had enough, he firmly smacked her bottom once. "Settle."

She let out a sharp cry of outrage. "I'm not a dog, alphan."

"Perhaps you would obey if you were." He laughed when she increased her struggles, finally setting her down when they were on the teleport pads. He took hold of her hand and pulled her close to him. "Hang on, Pei Ling." He doubted she'd teleported before.

Zafer held Pei Ling's hand tightly as they teleported to his spaceship, a sleek vessel that was his home during his rotation on Earth. He led her to the living quarters. He gestured for her to sit, but she remained standing, arms crossed over her chest.

"I don't want to be here," she said, her tone defiant.

"I understand that, but you agreed to the genetic modifications and mating. This is where we'll begin."

Pei Ling sighed, her shoulders slumping. "I know. I just...I didn't expect it to be like this."

Zafer frowned. "Like what?"

"Like being taken against my will, injected with some strange drug, and then forced to mate with an alien I barely know," she said, her voice trembling. "I feel like a...a broodmare."

Zafer felt a pang of guilt. He hadn't meant to make her feel like that. "I apologize if I made you feel that way. I'll do my best to make you comfortable."

Pei Ling nodded, but her expression remained guarded.

Zafer decided to give her some space and left the room, closing the door behind him. He wandered around the ship, checking on various systems, but his mind kept going back to Pei Ling. He couldn't blame her for being scared and wary. He had chosen her for her genetic compatibility, but he hadn't considered the emotional toll it would take on her.

A while later, he found her in the galley area, staring at a vidscreen that displayed Earth's current news. He cleared his throat to announce his presence, and she turned to face him. "Hungry?" he asked, gesturing to the synthicator.

Pei Ling shook her head. "No, thank you."

Zafer poured himself a glass of water and leaned against the counter. "I know this is difficult for you, but I hope you understand I didn't choose you lightly. I've wanted a child for a long time, and you matched best with an alphan. I have first choice, and I chose you because of your health, beauty, and genetic markers."

Pei Ling raised an eyebrow. "So, I'm just a walking incubator to you?"

Zafer bristled at her words but tried to remain calm. "No. You're the future mother of my child. That's an important and respected role in my culture."

Pei Ling snorted. "I'm sure it is."

Zafer took a deep breath, trying to keep his temper in check. "I understand you're angry and scared, but I hope you'll give me a chance to prove I'm not your enemy."

Pei Ling looked away, her expression softening. "I'm sorry. It's just...this is all so overwhelming."

Zafer nodded. "I'm sure it is." They fell into a slightly uncomfortable silence, but he found himself relaxing in her company. Perhaps she wasn't as spoiled as he had initially thought, but rather, she was scared and defensive. He wondered what her life had been like before he'd found her. "May I ask you something?"

Pei Ling looked at him warily. "What?"

"What was your life like before I found you?"

Pei Ling hesitated for a moment before speaking. "When the vorathans first invaded, I was ten and lived in Singapore. We were blessed in many ways, and my father used our wealth to buy a spot in a bunker in what used to be Wyoming. It's where we weathered much of the invasion."

Zafer nodded to indicate he was listening.

"We had everything we needed in the bunker. Food, water, medicine, and even entertainment. It wasn't until the government found us and took us out that I realized what life on Earth had become. I was shocked at the devastation and destruction and people suffering."

"I see. So, you were sheltered from much of the war?"

She nodded. "Yes. We had everything we needed in the bunker until almost six months ago when the government found us and claimed all the young women eligible for the draft. They arrested our parents for sheltering us, and I haven't seen my mom, dad, sister, or brother since. They took us to a processing center and explained the situation to us."

He felt a pang of sympathy. "That must have been difficult for you."

She shrugged. "I didn't really understand what was going on at first, but they gave me the datapad with all the information after you and I spoke. I was afraid, so I ran. I didn't know how to take care of myself, but I met Brighton, and she explained everything to me. She helped me adjust to life outside the bunker and taught me how to survive on my own."

Zafer nodded, impressed. "Brighton sounds like a good friend."

A small smile graced her lips. "She is. She took me in and helped me when she didn't have to. She had to be a broodmare though, so she left three months ago."

Zafer felt a twinge of annoyance at her phrasing of Brighton fulfilling her duty, but he pushed it aside. He had to focus on building a connection with her and proving he was a worthy mate. "I'm glad you had someone to help you."

Her eyes were sad. "The last three months have been frightening, and I started feeling watched."

He shifted slightly. "I paid a number of sources to look for you. I imagine you were being watched."

She glared for a moment but then sighed. "I guess this is inevitable. I shouldn't have tried to run."

He didn't like how she sounded like a sacrificial lamb, but he didn't want to argue with her. "As I said, I won't hurt you."

"I'm scared of this omegan thing and the heat cycle."

"I'll be here with you." He shifted. "Honestly, I haven't been through it either. There aren't many alphans left, male or female, and the few I've met were either already mated or incapable of entering an omegan phase. The mosaics tried to help us solve that problem, but it seemed most of us with an omegan ability died between the vorathans invading our solar system and diseases that ran rampant in the aftermath. Most alphans can only impregnate, not be impregnated, now."

She blinked. "Even your females?"

He nodded. "Alphans need a partner who can enter an omegan heat cycle. When that happens, the alphans enter our alphan cycle, and we're a compatible match. Otherwise, sex is for pleasure, not reproduction. Only during a heat can an alphan with an omegan gene become pregnant. Mosaics found it impossible to manipulate our genome enough to make some alphans acquire the omegan gene without changing our very species. It's easier to adapt human women and men, for some reason."

"Lucky me," she said with a hint of bitterness before sighing. "I'll do my best to give you what you expect, Zafer."

He inclined his head. "I'll do my best to make you happy during the process." It was his silent wish that she'd choose to stay with him, but he wasn't going to put much hope in that when thirty percent of proxy surrogates walked away at the end of the year or the end of a pregnancy. He couldn't pretend he didn't want her to stay, but he wouldn't tell her that unless or until he thought they had some sort of true connection.

"What about you? What was your life like before the vorathans?"

He blinked, trying to remember. "I was a small boy when they invaded my planet. There were six planets in the alphan solar system, and five supported life. I lived on Alpha Three, which was a colony world. I remember a large city, beautiful art my mother always admired and tried to imitate, and being happy." He flinched as he recalled the invasion.

It had started with dozens of explosions and flashes of lights. His parents had probably been aware of what was happening, but neither he nor his siblings had any indication of the situation until the actual invasion. "It was terrifying to a small child. I hid in my toy chest. That was where the Faction soldiers found me two days later, when they came to search for survivors."

Pei Ling listened intently, sympathy in her eyes. "I'm sorry. That must have been horrible."

He nodded. "I was lucky to be found by the Faction. I've been with them ever since. They've been my family since I was a child."

She reached out and touched his arm. "You've been through so much."

He shrugged. "It was a long time ago. I've had a good life, despite the war and the loss of my family. I had a chance to live, unlike most of the people I knew in my life before, and I'm grateful for that."

She blinked, looking on the verge of tears. "I've never known loss like that. I've been sheltered and privileged my whole life."

He understood her guilt, and he didn't want her to feel ashamed of her upbringing. "That doesn't mean you haven't faced battles of your own. Everyone's struggles are different."

She smiled slightly, and he felt a spark of connection between them. Maybe, just maybe, they could build something together. For now, he was content to keep getting to know her and building trust.

Chapter Two

Pei Ling

PEI LING LOOKED AROUND the spacious room, marveling at the technological advancements that were unlike anything she'd known in the bunker. Zafer had been gracious enough to give her a quick tour of his starship, showing her different rooms and compartments, but now they were back at the living space, which had to be shared quarters. There wasn't enough space on the starship to have another bedroom tucked away somewhere.

The room was well-lit, and everything looked so clean and organized, unlike the cramped POD she had been living in before. It was also larger than the bunker room she'd shared with her sister, Mei.

"Here we are," said Zafer, gesturing to the room. "This is where you'll be staying for the next year."

Pei Ling nodded, still taking in the new environment. "It's...big." It had to account for about a fifth of the entire ship.

Zafer chuckled. "Yes, it's a bit different from what you're used to, I imagine. A Faction warrior mostly lives on his ship as part of the larger armada, so we have to have everything we need contained within. I hope you'll be comfortable here."

She nodded. "Thank you, Zafer. I really appreciate everything you've done for me." Her tone was sincere. She was still worried, but he seemed gentle and undemanding, which was the best she could hope for in such a situation.

He smiled warmly. "Of course. I want you to feel safe and happy."

They fell into a comfortable silence, and Pei Ling walked around the room, examining the different gadgets and devices scattered throughout. She noticed a door leading to what looked like a bedroom and paused, unsure what to do.

Zafer seemed to sense her hesitation. "That's the bedroom. I won't go in there unless you're comfortable with it."

Pei Ling nodded, grateful for his consideration. "Thank you."

He sat down on a nearby couch and gestured for her to join him. "Would you like to watch a movie?"

She grinned, happy to have a distraction from her worries. "We had movie nights twice a week in the bunker, and we never watched the same one twice. What do you have?"

He pulled up a holographic menu and scrolled through the options. "How about this one? It's a recent Earth release. Hollywood is slowly getting back in business."

She sat down beside him, snuggling into the couch cushions. As the movie started playing, she found herself relaxing more and more, grateful for this moment of peace and normalcy amidst the chaos of her life.

Unfortunately, the movie wasn't all that peaceful. It was about a mother searching for her lost child in the days after the vorathan invasion. By the time she found her son at the end of the movie, alive but traumatized, Pei Ling was crying softly.

"Are you well?" He seemed worried.

She nodded. "Is this a true story?"

He looked at the holographic menu for a moment. "It doesn't say."

"Even if it isn't, I'm sure there were a lot of stories like this. I..." She trailed off, unable to explain why she was crying so hard. Perhaps it was the understanding of why her government had agreed to the Faction's terms for protection. Was it so terrible to give up a year of her life to save millions of lives? It was confusing, and it made her question everything she'd taken for granted until now.

He reached out a tentative hand to touch her leg. "I'm sorry. It wasn't my intent to upset you."

She nodded again, finally gaining control of her emotions. "I know. Perhaps I overreacted, but I haven't really seen firsthand the days after the invasion. Just the aftermath years later. It would have been so much worse if the Faction didn't come, wouldn't it?"

He nodded without hesitation. "The vorathans left fewer than ten percent of the alphan population alive with their invasion of my world's five planets. There were ten billion of us before the vorathans. That's just one society of the many they've brutalized over the millennia."

"I guess Earth didn't see much of a choice when the Faction offered to help."

"We prevented a lot of bloodshed, but I'm sorry women in your generation and beyond have to pay the tab." He stroked her knee. "If I were noble enough to let you go, another would claim you. It's the reality in which we live now."

She nodded slowly. "My fate seems far better now than it would have been if the Faction hadn't arrived."

"Most likely."

They sat in comfortable silence for a few moments before Pei Ling spoke up. "Can I contact Brighton to let her know I'm okay?"

He nodded. "Of course. I'll set up a communication channel for you."

She leaned forward excitedly. "Thank you. I haven't been able to talk to her since...well, since she left for the Embassy to meet her Brundle commander."

He got up from the couch, moving toward the control panel. "I'll set it up right now."

As he worked on setting up the communication channel, she waited with a touch of impatience and eagerness, wanting to see how Brighton was faring in her mating and hoped her friend was content. Did she have a good man like Zafer?

The thought startled her, but she couldn't deny its truth. Despite their differences, she was starting to see him as more than just an alien captor. He seemed to genuinely care about her well-being, and while she was still afraid of the mysterious omegan heat cycle, she was less afraid now that she knew more about him. She couldn't imagine him hurting her.

"The system is ready. Communications on Baxa can be spotty, but I believe I've found the right Brundle...Dantel Oleig." He gestured her forward, quickly showing her how to work the vidscreen. "I'll leave you to your conversation and make some dinner with the synthicator, if you're hungry now?"

She nodded, her stomach rumbling slightly. "I'll join you shortly." When he'd gone, she pressed the "Connect" button, and a red alien with a muzzle and long golden hair answered a few moments later. The connection was staticky.

"Yes?" He sounded abrupt.

"I...may I speak with Brighton?"

He grunted and called for her, sounding grumpy. Pei Ling was instantly afraid for her friend, and when Brighton's red-gold head appeared in the vidscreen before she turned to face her, she couldn't help asking, "Is he as mean as he sounds?"

Brigthon blinked and then laughed. "No. It's the muzzle. It gives him a bit of growliness." Then she smiled. "I've been worried about you, Pei Ling. How are you?"

Pei Ling smiled back, warmth spread through her chest. "I'm doing okay. I'm settling onto Zafer's ship now."

Brighton's eyebrows lifted in surprise. "Who's Zafer?"

That required a bit of explanation, since she hadn't told her friend she was running from a mating, or why she'd been scavenging on the street.

Once she explained, Brighton seemed worried about her. "He kidnapped you?"

She nodded and then shook her head, feeling a bit defensive. "Not exactly. He found me and claimed me as his omegan mate after I ran, but he's been kind to me, and I feel safe with him."

Brighton's expression softened. "I'm glad you're safe. You deserve to be with someone who'll take care of you."

Pei Ling felt a lump form in her throat. "Thank you. How are things with you and Dantel?"

Brighton's smile widened, and she turned to say something to Dantel offscreen before turning back to Pei Ling. "Things are going well actually. He's not so bad once you get to know him, though there's a head on my wall..." She trailed off with a giggle before explaining that.

She was happy to see her friend happy, though she didn't know if she could have accepted a head on her wall. "I miss you though."

"I miss you too. Are you coming to Baxa?"

She hesitated. "I believe Zafer's rotation will last for another year, so he and I won't be together then unless I'm pregnant. The Chief Medical Officer assures me I'll likely be pregnant with the first heat, so I'll be back on Earth when he leaves for Baxa." Why did that thought leave her aching with regret?

Brighton frowned but didn't point out she and her two friends had been lucky enough to find mates in their matches. "Stay in touch wherever you are."

"I will. You too." After ending the vidcall, she left the living space to find Zafer in the galley. She was out of sorts and not sure how to proceed, but when she entered the room, she immediately felt calmer just being around him. It boded well for their partnership, but she cautioned herself not to get attached or expect too much. She wanted to return to her family and make sure they were safe, not go live on an alien world. Right?

Chapter Three

Pei Ling

IN THE TEN DAYS SHE'D been with him, she discovered he had a way of making her feel safe, welcomed, and appreciated without any expectations. He'd been kind and considerate to her, so she couldn't understand why she was so bitchy with him the last two days.

"Would you like chicken for dinner?"

"No. I want beef. We just had chicken."

Later, when they'd been watching an old movie. "Do you need extra an extra blanket? You seem cold."

"I'm burning up."

And just a few hours ago. "I'm going to be on the bridge for my shift, so please don't bother me unless it's an emergency."

That had caused her to burst into tears. "I sure don't want to be an inconvenience to you, so I won't bother you."

He'd tiptoed out of the room, looking afraid, and she could hardly blame him. She was practically psychotic, and she suspected it had something to do with that shot. Quillin had said it would only cause side effects for a few hours, but it must be a delayed reaction.

She was on her way to place a vidcall to the Embassy and demand to speak to the Med Chief when a pain hit her stomach. It was low, tight, and clenching, making her feel like nothing she'd ever experienced before. She cried out and stood up, not sure what had happened. It wasn't exactly a pain. More like a fierce need for...something.

She couldn't decide what, and she paced frantically. It was impossible to focus on anything as a mad rush of sensations and conflicting ideas filled her, leaving her confused. "I need a nest." She muttered that aloud, and though it made no sense to her, she immediately went to the bed and started stripping the linens. She piled them into the corner in a heap and laid down in them. No, not quite.

She jumped up and went to the closet, removing everything soft she could find. When she was done, she had a pleasing nest on the floor, and she laid down again. That felt perfect, except her clothes were itchy and too restrictive. Without another thought, she stripped them off and laid down in the nest. She required...something. She couldn't identify it, but it was a fierce, aching need that she was sure would never be quenched.

The door to the bedroom opened suddenly, and Zafer stalked in. He stared at her with his eyes burning an intense blue. His nostrils flared, and he let out a primitive cry. Rather than scare her, it turned her on. She let out one in response, and it filtered through her mind that she must be entering heat. She didn't care and wasn't concerned with the particulars right then.

"Mate," he said in a growl. "Heat." He started tearing at his uniform with a frantic edge she recognized in herself. With those two words, he crossed the room and swept her into his arms, taking her straight to the nest she'd just made.

Pei Ling's breath caught in her throat as Zafer's lips ghosted over the sensitive skin of her neck. His hands roved over her body, caressing her curves gently despite the pent-up ferocity she sensed in him. His need was as great as hers, but he moved carefully. His touch sent sparks of electric pleasure through her body, and she shuddered in response.

Her body heated as his hands made their way down to her belly, exploring her belly button before they drifted down lower. "Your smell is driving me wild." He almost growled the words against her thigh as he inhaled. "You must taste divine." He pushed her onto her back, and his head moved between her legs, his tongue exploring her. She let out a whimper of need as his mouth caressed her dripping pussy before his lips parted her wider, and his tongue surged inside.

Pei Ling moaned as his tongue moved within her. She moaned in pleasure, which intensified with every dart and stroke. She gasped as the heat of his breath on her made her shudder. His tongue moved expertly, creating waves of pleasure that coursed through her veins, leaving both of them drenched with her slick. She grew hotter and wetter as he explored her deepest depths.

He kept up the rhythm, taking his time and savoring every moment until she was quivering beneath him with need. He teased and tantalized until she couldn't take it anymore, and then he moved to satisfy her. She came with a shout as her body clenched, and she tightened her thighs around his head.

He remained still against her, his tongue barely stroking her, until she was able to unclench her legs. Then, he started kissing her skin again as he worked his way up to find her mouth. Their first kiss was electrifying, sending shockwaves of pleasure through her entire body. She clung to him tightly, wanting...no, *needing* more.

She opened her eyes and looked into his. His blue eyes were dark and full of desire. Her own yearning soared higher at the sight of his. The orgasm he'd given her had barely taken off the edge. She wanted to feel his warmth as it spread through her body, igniting a passion she'd never felt before. "More." She sounded as inarticulate as him when the word came out as little more than a grunt.

He bent down, his lips claiming hers in another passionate kiss. His tongue explored her mouth, tasting her and claiming her as his own as the taste of her arousal lingered on the appendage. She gasped in pleasure as his tongue teased and tantalized her. This kiss lasted for what seemed like an eternity with their tongues dancing together in a ferocious embrace. Finally, He pulled away, but he kept his gaze on her. Her heart raced at the intensity of his gaze.

He ran a hand down her body before he spoke. "I want to be inside you," he said, his voice low and intense, "But I don't want to frighten you."

Her eyes widened. "I've had only pleasure so far."

"I hope that continues. My cock is large, and I understand you will be tight, especially as a virgin. I have to warn you about my knot…"

She whimpered, shifting restlessly and wrapping her thighs around his waist. "Just show me. I need you, Zafer."

He seemed to hesitate before surrendering with a groan. She looked into his eyes and saw determination there, along with desire. He tightened his hold and brought her hips upward, so her sheath cradled the tip of his cock. It was smooth and cylindrical, without a differentiation between head and shaft, but she didn't notice much else when he kissed her again, his hands caressing her body as he explored her.

Her passion rose, blotting out logical thought, as her body responded to his touch. His hands continued to move over her, caressing and exploring as his hips canted forward.

When his cock entered her, giving her the rest of his shaft, she stiffened. "It hurts."

He growled and kissed her forehead. "Stop?"

She shook her head. "No." She couldn't bear the thought of him severing this connection in spite of the pain. He began to slowly thrust in and out of her, and the shape of his cock made his possession easier. Once the pain faded, she felt only pleasure consuming her.

They arched together, building up a frantic rhythm. She strained toward release as he grunted and bucked his hips, filling every inch of her pussy. She came with a cry, saying, "Zafer," over and over again.

He stiffened, his shaft spasming as jets of his release filled her. He let out a guttural growl as his cock grew inside her instead of softening.

Her eyes widened as panic filled her. "What's happening?"

"My knot." He sounded hoarse. "It keeps us together for a while."

She slowly relaxed, adjusting to his knot inside her. To her surprise, her body quivered in pleasure as she climaxed a few more times just from him knotting her. He seemed to be coming again too, but it was hard to tell as her body shook with pleasure. Zafer's body tensed with one last surge as his knotting completed the process that bound them together before it began to soften.

For a moment, she was suspended in a flash of bliss. Eventually, the pleasure began to subside as the knot slowly disappeared, and his shaft returned to its former size and shape.

Zafer rolled off her and pulled her into his arms. She was secure in his arms, with her body still humming with pleasure.

He kissed her forehead and pulled her close, holding her tightly against his body as they sank into the nest she'd made purely on instinct. Her body still thrummed with satisfaction. She closed her eyes and allowed herself to drift off into a peaceful sleep, safe in his arms.

She woke later to him frantically taking her again, and she enjoyed every second. She was exhausted though and fell asleep with his knot still inside her. When she woke a third time, she was still bound to him. "Again?" she asked in a teasing tone.

He looked pensive. "Still. There is a stage of mating that can last up to twelve hours. I wanted to tell you all this before, but I couldn't hold back. I'm sorry."

She purred and shifted slightly to enjoy his knot more fully. "It's okay. I told you to show me."

"Mmhmm." He still looked uncertain. "I promised not to enter the bedroom unless you felt comfortable, but when I smelled your heat, I became like a man possessed."

She smiled. "It's okay. I was feeling a similar level of need. Still do, actually." Having his knot inside her seemed to stir her desire continuously rather than abating it. No wonder the Med Chief thought they'd be pregnant by the time their first mating ended. How could she not be? "I'm sorry too."

"For what?" He was frowning.

"I was a raging bitch the last couple of days. I didn't realize I was going into heat, but I tend to get moody before my menses, so I guess it's like that, times a thousand."

"I barely noticed." He almost said that with a straight face.

She laughed. "Sure." She snuggled closer as he began to thrust into her. With them locked together, it was more of a rocking sensation, since he couldn't move much, but it satisfied what her body craved. "You seem pretty diplomatic. Are you sure you haven't been a mate before?"

"Never." He held her closer. "You're my first...only..."

Her eyes misted at the words. They could just be from the passion of the moment, but she wanted to believe them. She wanted to cling to him and feel claimed for more than just a year. She wanted him for the rest of her life. That could be the incredible sex influencing her, but she thought it was more than that.

Chapter Four

Zafer

SEVERAL DAYS LATER, Pei Ling sat on the couch, scrolling through the holo-library on her datapad. She looked up when Zafer walked into the living area, a small smile playing on her lips.

"What are you up to?" he asked, crossing the room to sit next to her. He breathed in her scent, which still intoxicated him though her heat had passed days before.

"Just looking for something to do," she said, holding up her datapad. "I've read everything in the ship's library twice over, and I'm starting to get bored."

He chuckled. "I can't say I'm surprised. Living in a confined space for weeks on end can do that to a person. How about I teach you to fly the ship?" As he made the impulsive offer, he silently cursed himself. What an idiotic thing to suggest.

Her eyes lit up. "Really? You'd do that?"

Zafer hesitated. "It's against a billion regulations, and if we're caught, we could both get in a lot of trouble, but I can't deny my omegan anything, and you're starting to get restless."

Pei Ling beamed at him. "I promise I won't tell anyone."

Zafer shook his head. "It's not about you telling anyone. It's about the ship's sensors picking up an unauthorized user."

"I understand," said Pei Ling, nodding eagerly. "Can we do it anyway? Just for a little while?"

He sighed, realizing he'd brought this on himself. "All right, but we have to be careful. I'll show you the basics, but I'll be right there with you the whole time."

Her smile widened. "Thank you. This is going to be amazing."

A short time later, he watched Pei Ling closely as she piloted the ship, taking them through the starry expanse between Earth and the Moon. She was a natural, her movements smooth and confident. He felt a swell of pride in her and couldn't help but smile. "You're doing great," he said, his voice warm and encouraging.

She grinned. "Thanks. I never thought I'd be able to do something like this."

"You're a natural."

She looked up at him, her eyes shining with gratitude. "The view is incredible, and having you here is equally amazing."

A surge of affection for her threatened to overwhelm him. He enjoyed spending time with her and talking to her, learning more about her with each passing day. They had become close, and he felt a sense of protectiveness, and possessiveness, toward her that he couldn't deny.

As the days had passed, they'd spent more time together, talking and laughing, and he began to care more and more for her. The thought of leaving her behind on Earth when their time was over and he went to Baxa, hopefully with a baby, nearly gutted him. He didn't want to pressure her, so he kept the thoughts to himself, but he couldn't help hoping she'd choose to stay with him.

He cleared his throat, trying to clear his thoughts. "We'd better dock with the spaceport. If we fly much longer, it might alert the Faction systems."

Her face fell, but she didn't protest. She turned the ship around and flew them back to the dock. Before he could say he'd take over for that crucial step, she snugged them against the docking socket, and they heard the sound of it coupling with the ship a moment later.

He exhaled loudly, realizing he'd been holding his breath. "Like I said...a natural. It took me weeks to master that maneuver in flight training."

She grinned, bouncing out of the seat. "That was so amazing." She threw herself into his arms, hugging him tightly.

He automatically held onto her, tightening his embrace as he breathed in her scent. "Amazing." He wasn't referring to the short flight.

She pulled back slowly, her expression serious. "May I ask you something?"

"Of course."

"I...I know we're different, you and I, but...I feel like we have a connection. Is that crazy?"

Zafer's heart skipped a beat at her words. He'd felt it too but had been hesitant to admit it. "It's not crazy at all. I feel it too."

Her eyes were wide with hope and a touch of wariness. "You do?"

He nodded, his hand reaching out to brush a strand of hair from her face. "I care for you more than I ever thought possible."

Her dark eyes softened as her lips curved into a smile that showed no trace of hesitation. "I care for you too. I never thought I could feel this way about an alien I was forced to be with, because I was so afraid, especially of the omegan cycle. Who knew that would be such an amazing four days?" She gave him a suggestive look, relaying with her gaze that she wanted him again. "I want to do that over and over."

Zafer leaned in closer, his heart pounding. They couldn't get pregnant with sex like this, but he wasn't about to say no. "It might not last four days, but I can pleasure you any time you wish."

Pei Ling's smile grew wider, her eyes shining. "I believe you, Zafer. And...I'm not afraid anymore. I definitely wish." She licked her lips and winked.

Zafer exhaled in relief. He'd been afraid she would never fully trust him, but now he knew she did. They had a connection that went beyond their species and cultural differences, and it was something special. He leaned in and brushed his lips against hers, his heart racing with emotion. Soon enough, he lifted and carried her into their bedroom. He'd been sleeping beside her since her heat ended.

The nest she'd made was gone, and the bed was back to being neatly made, though they soon mussed the covers. They made love as humans would, or alphans not trying to breed, and he loved it almost as much as he had when he was buried inside her, tied together by his knot, and feeling like they were the only two beings in the multiverse.

HE HATED TO LEAVE HER, but he was called for a briefing a couple of weeks later. He found her preparing food from the synthicator and sat at the galley table. "I have to go to the Embassy tomorrow for a few hours."

She frowned and turned to give him a tray. "Must you?"

He nodded reluctantly. "I wish I could avoid it, but I can't. It's a mandatory briefing, and it must be in person because of sensitive data. Would you like to come with me and wait at the Embassy?"

After a hesitation, she shook her head. "There's not much for me to do at the Embassy. I think I'll stay here."

He nodded his acceptance of her decision, and they ate. That night, he made love to her again, feeling a softening inside her core. She might be about to enter another heat cycle, though it was a little soon for that. Humans induced to be omegans could have unpredictable cycles though.

He rolled out of bed early the next morning. She clung to him for a moment, half-asleep. He kissed her forehead. "I have to go, remember?"

She opened her eyes and nodded. "Yes. Come back soon."

"I'll do what I can." He gave her a lingering kiss, resisting the urge to get back in the bed, and pulled away. "I'll see you soon."

She murmured something sleepily and snuggled back into the covers.

He left to do his duty, spending hours at the Embassy before teleporting back to the spaceport, where he'd docked his ship. He returned home as quickly as he could, calling, "Pei Ling, I'm back."

There was no response. He looked around the ship, but she was nowhere to be found. Panic started to rise in his chest. Had she run away again? He checked his communication device and saw there were several missed communiques from the Faction. He immediately called into the Central Command Hub.

"Zafer," said a male voice on the other end of the line, "We've been trying to reach you. Your human mate arrived at the Embassy, but then she left quickly. She's on the surface."

"What? When did this happen?" Why would she go to the Embassy? Was she looking for him? If so, it made no sense for her to leave the Embassy and go out into the city...unless she was running again.

"She left a few hours after you departed for the Embassy. We've been trying to contact her, but she's not responding. We've tracked her to a location on the planet's surface. We're sending you the coordinates now."

Zafer's heart sank. "Thank you." She must be trying to leave him. For a moment, he was tempted to allow her to do it if she wanted so badly to be free, but he couldn't. Not without knowing why she was leaving him when he thought they'd connected and had admitted their feelings last night. Had it all been a ruse to make him complacent?

After he ended the call, he called up the coordinates to transfer to his ship and wrist comm. Maybe he'd let her go if she could explain why she didn't want to stay. It felt like ripping out his own heart, but how could he force her to remain with him if she was unhappy? His mind was racing with thoughts of Pei Ling and what could have driven her to leave. He couldn't deny he was hurt and angry that she'd left without telling him.

He went straight to the bridge, his mind in turmoil, though he'd run through the process of takeoff so often his muscle memory carried him through the task. As he started the engines and prepared to leave, he couldn't shake the certainty she'd run from him. He had been a gentle alphan mate, giving her space and never pushing her beyond her comfort zone. Now, with her gone and with no explanation, he was prepared to be a forceful and demanding alphan if necessary. He couldn't let her run away again. Not when they had grown so close. Not without understanding her thought processes.

Not without convincing her to change her mind? He clung to that hope as he navigated from the spaceport and directed his ship toward the surface. The search would be more efficient with his shuttle instead of a skid.

The journey to the surface felt like it took forever. Worry and fear for Pei Ling consumed his thoughts, along with a strong dash of hurt and confusion. What if she were hurt? What if someone had taken her? His heart raced as he landed the ship at the coordinates given to him by the Faction.

He looked around, surprised to find himself in some sort of shanty town. It was definitely on the outskirts of human civilization. It was where those wanting to evade the Earth government and drop out of human society sought refuge together. Why was she here?

As he stepped out of the ship, there was movement in the distance. He approached cautiously, ready for anything. As two people came into view—a man and a woman—he increased his pace. He was sure the woman ahead of him was Pei Ling. She had the same stature and shoulder-length blue-black hair.

He broke into a run and was unable to slow himself when he heard the sound of a pulser charging. With a flash of light from the muzzle, it crossed the distance between him and the two figures, striking him. Pain exploded through his body, and he cried out and staggered forward, trying to keep his balance.

Instead, he fell to the ground, trying to catch his breath. Figures moved toward him, but everything was blurry.

Chapter Five

Pei Ling
A few hours ago...

IT WAS PERFECT. SHE nearly giggled to herself when he told her he was leaving. "Do you want to come with me?" he asked.

It would be a perfect time, but she wanted it all to be a surprise. "No, I think I'll just stay here."

When she woke the next day after their sleepy morning parting, he was gone. She was disappointed but also excited, because now was her chance. She bathed and dressed quickly before joining the queue at the spaceport to teleport to Earth. She half-expected someone to challenge her right to travel freely, since she'd been a runaway proxy, but no one seemed to care when she presented the ID card she'd received at the Embassy.

She was on her way to Medbay when her wrist comm chirped. She expected it to be Zafer since no one else she knew had the frequency. Pei Ling answered the call, anticipating hearing her mate on the other end.

Instead, it was her brother's panicked voice that greeted her. "Thank goodness I finally got hold of you, Pei Ling."

She stumbled for a moment and frowned at the wrist comm as a hazy picture of her brother filled the small screen. "Bai? How did you get this frequency?"

"I've been paying someone who works at the Embassy to monitor when you or Mei return to Earth."

Mei wasn't on Earth either? She worried immediately for her little sister, wondering if she'd also been paired with an alphan, since sisters must have similar DNA. "What's going on, Bai?"

"Dad has collapsed. You need to come right away. He's on electronic release and being monitored by the Bighorn Detention Center, along with Mom. We're in a...settlement nearby."

Her heart sank at the news. She'd been planning to visit Medbay, but that could wait. She had to go see her father. "I'm on my way," she said, already turning around to leave Medbay. "Bighorn is almost a thousand miles away. I'll have to catch one of the Faction shuttles, but I'll get there as soon as I can."

"Just hurry. There isn't much time."

"Of course." After ending the call, she tried to send a message to Zafer to let him know what was happening. She wanted him to be with her, though she doubted he could get away from his briefing.

As she rushed from the Embassy, still composing the message, she hit Send. The indicator turned red after a moment, so she tried again. She tried again and again, but each attempt failed. After multiple tries, she realized it wasn't going to go through. In her haste to leave the Embassy, she must have overlooked some important step in the communication process.

Pei Ling's stomach twisted with nausea, which had become a frequent occurrence the last few days, but this felt like unease. She had no way of letting Zafer know what was happening, and she didn't know how long she would be gone. He'd be worried, and she felt guilty for leaving without telling him, but her father's health was more important right now. It sounded like he was critical, and if her father was dying, she had to be there for him.

Setting the communication to continuously try to deliver, she walked a few blocks to a shuttle hub, buying a ticket for the Bighorn sector. The lines were long, and people were impatient, but she didn't let it phase her. She was focused on getting to her father.

SEVERAL HOURS LATER, feeling tired, hungry, and anxious, Pei Ling arrived at the coordinates Bai had given her, expecting to find a hospital or medical facility. Instead, she saw a series of rundown buildings, looking more like a makeshift refugee camp than anything else. She called out for her brother, feeling increasingly anxious as she looked around at the desperate-looking people milling about.

Suddenly, Bai appeared from behind a nearby building, wearing a backpack and carrying a large duffel bag. "Pei Ling, over here," he called out, waving his arms to get her attention.

She rushed over to him, noticing his nervous expression and the way his eyes darted. "What's going on, Bai? Where's Dad?"

"We have to leave now," he said, grabbing her arm and pulling her along. "I've arranged transport for all of us off Earth, but first, we have to get out of here. I've paid some pirates to acquire Mei and bring her to our new home. I've rescued you, and she'll soon be safe too."

Pei Ling stopped in her tracks, trying to pull her arm out of Bai's grasp. "What? No, Bai, I don't want to be *rescued*. What's going on?"

Bai looked at her with concern in his eyes. "It's complicated, but our parents won't go without you and Mei, and I've managed to find Mei too thanks to my contact inside the alien Embassy. We should go now."

Go? Pei Ling's heart sank at the sight of her brother's backpack and duffel bag. It was clear he'd been planning this for a while, and he'd come prepared. Her mind raced as she tried to make sense of what was happening. "Bai, please tell me what's going on. Why do we have to leave?"

Bai looked around nervously before he turned to her with a serious expression. "Because I said so. I've arranged transport for all of us off Earth. First, we have to get out of here. I've paid some pirates to acquire Mei, since she's enroute to Baxa with her alien abductor."

Pei Ling's heart lurched at the mention of her sister being in danger. "What do you mean, 'alien abductor?' Mei is with an alien?"

Bai nodded, his expression darkening. "Yes, an alphan, so you must know what she's going through."

She frowned. "It's not what you think, Bai. She's not being hurt, if that's what you fear. I promise."

He scowled. "You've clearly succumbed to Stockholm Syndrome, but I'm going to save both of you and our parents. And myself. I'm not accepting any amount of enticement to submit myself to an alphan female."

"What?" She tried to pull away from him. "What do you mean?"

"Men aren't drafted, but some aliens think we can be bought. You and Mei matching to alphans generated interest in me. I'm not going to sell myself into sexual slavery to be some omegan to an alphan. I'm saving all of us from that fate and our parents from prison for the *terrible* crime of protecting us first from the vorathans and then the government."

"We can't just leave like this."

He glared at her, shaking her arm roughly. Her brother appeared genuinely terrified. "It's not safe for any of us here. We must go now before it's too late."

Pei Ling's mind was spinning as she tried to process what Bai was saying. She didn't want to leave Zafer or the life they were building together. Assuming her sister's match was as gentle as Zafer, Mei wasn't in danger, but Bai refused to believe that. She had to do something, but she didn't know what.

"Where do you want to go?" she asked, trying to keep her voice calm.

"To a safer place than Earth. I've converted most of the family fortune I could get my hands on to rathium, and we can afford to start over," said Bai, grabbing her arm and pulling her along with him.

Pei Ling stumbled, her heart pounding in her chest. "No, Bai," she protested, trying to pull away, "I can't leave Zafer. He's my mate."

Bai turned to her, his expression stern. "I'm sorry, but you don't have a choice. Our parents won't leave without you and Mei. We *are* leaving."

Pei Ling's heart sank at the realization her brother wasn't going to listen to her. She had to think of something, but she didn't know what. As he tried to drag her forward through the maze of rundown buildings, she dug in her heels and attempted to think of a way out of the situation. She couldn't just abandon Zafer. She understood his need to get their parents somewhere safe, where they wouldn't face a prison sentence for taking care of their family, but she couldn't leave her mate.

"Stop fighting me." He shook her again, making her bite her tongue. "You're brainwashed, but I'm trying to help you."

She started to argue with him, but a figure stepped out from behind a nearby building. It was Zafer. Pei Ling's heart leaped with joy at the sight of him, but then her brother pulled out a gun and aimed it at the blue alien.

She froze in shock as Bai fired the gun, acting only at the last second to divert his aim. That led to him hitting Zafer in the shoulder instead of the chest. Her brother was distracted by her interference, and as he tugged the gun away from her to aim again, she took the opportunity to hit him on the head with a nearby piece of metal. "I'm sorry," she whispered as he slumped to the ground, unconscious.

Rushing to Zafer's side, Pei Ling used his wrist comm to have the Embassy teleport them away. She was worried he wouldn't be okay, but he woke up as they materialized in the Embassy's Medbay.

"Pei Ling?" He groaned, looking around in confusion. "What happened?"

She helped him sit up, her eyes filled with tears of relief. "We were attacked, but we're safe now." Her voice was shaking from reaction and suppressed tears.

His eyes widened in concern. "Attacked? Are you hurt?"

She shook her head, her eyes filling with tears. "No, I'm okay, but you were shot."

He grimaced as he looked down at his shoulder. "I'll be okay. It's just a flesh wound." He looked more closely at her. "Who attacked us, and why did you leave me?"

Pei Ling's heart sank at the disappointment in Zafer's voice. She had a lot of explaining to do, but she was relieved to see he was going to be okay. "It was my brother, Bai," she said, taking a deep breath. "He wanted to take us off Earth to keep our parents safe, but I couldn't leave you."

His expression softened as he reached out to take her hand. "I understand. I might do the same if it was my family, but why didn't you tell me?"

She looked down, wallowing in guilt. "I tried to send you a message, but it didn't go through." She lifted her wrist to shake the comm. "I'll have to download the log to prove it to you, but I put the message on continuous send so it might eventually go through."

"I believe you," he said gruffly, though his gaze was filled with concern. "We need to report this to the Faction. They need to know what's going on."

Her heart sank as she shook her head. "The Faction will report them to Earth's government, and they're the ones holding my parents for trial. I know they didn't do the right thing in the government's eyes by trying to hide me, Mei, and the other women eligible for the draft, but they'd already taken us down there to protect us from the vorathan invasion. They were just continuing to protect us. My parents shouldn't have to go to prison for that."

Zafer's expression softened as he placed a gentle hand on her shoulder. "I understand what you're saying, but we can't let your brother get away with what he's done. He shot me without cause, and that's a serious offense."

Pei Ling sighed, knowing he was right. "I just don't want my family to suffer anymore. We've been through enough already."

Zafer leaned in closer to her, his voice quiet and comforting. "I'll do everything in my power to make sure your family is safe." He looked pained as he admitted, "Your parents will probably serve time in prison. The Faction keeps their laws separate from Earth's whenever possible, and they broke Earth law by sheltering you all. I don't know if I know anyone powerful enough who'd be willing to intercede on their behalf."

"They were saving us."

"Yes, and there's probably some resentment that they were able to use their wealth to save their family, just like all the other bunker families, while everyone else suffered during the invasion, the war, and afterward. That's how humans think, isn't it? Some aliens too. They'll want to punish them for not enduring the same suffering as everyone else."

She nodded slowly. "I know they didn't do the right thing, but they thought it was right for us."

"I know." He kissed her forehead as Quillin approached. "I'll try to intercede, but I won't lie and pretend I can do much."

She nodded slowly, blinking rapidly as she tried to hide her pain at what her parents faced. Justified or not, she couldn't imagine them enduring prison and more ridicule because they'd protected their families. She doubt any other human in a similar position would have declined the opportunity to keep themselves safe from the invasion and aftermath.

The Med Chief arrived then. "Didn't I see you earlier today, Pei Ling?" He asked that as he ran a sensor over Zafer's shoulder. "You were at the doorway and then rushed out."

The wound started to heal before her eyes. "Uh, yeah."

Zafer looked concerned. "What? Why were you coming to Medbay, and why didn't you tell me?"

She gave him a wobbly smile. "I wanted it to be a surprise..." With that, the events of the day caught up with her, and she swooned straight into his arms.

47

Chapter Six

Zafer

ZAFER WAS CONFUSED at first when Pei Ling told him what had happened. He'd thought she had left him willingly and had been hurt by her sudden departure. Then he'd listened intently as she explained the situation with her family and the danger they were in. He couldn't blame her for wanting to protect her loved ones, but he couldn't condone her brother's actions either.

When she suddenly fainted into his arms, panic filled him. He quickly laid her down on the nearest exam table and moved aside for Quillin to examine her. He watched anxiously as the Med Chief ran a sensor over her body to check her vital signs.

He stood beside her, holding her hand tightly as he watched the Med Chief's face for any sign of concern.

After a few moments, Quillin straightened, his expression softening. "She's okay, Zafer," he said, his voice calm. "She's just exhausted. I'll give her something to help her sleep, and we'll monitor her closely."

Zafer breathed a sigh of relief, his heart racing as he looked down at his mate's pale face. He brushed a strand of blue-black hair away from her forehead. Her eyelids fluttered. "Are you okay, my love?"

She opened her eyes, looking up at him with a small smile. "I'm okay," she said, her voice weak. "Just tired."

Quillin turned to Zafer with a smile. "There's something else, Zafer. Pei Ling is pregnant."

His heart leaped with joy at the news, and he had to blink back tears. "A baby?" He sounded like he was choking on his emotions for a moment, until he coughed. "We're having a baby?"

Pei Ling nodded, and her eyes were bright with tears. "Yes. I thought I was, so I wanted to make sure and then surprise you with the news."

Zafer leaned down, kissing her gently on the lips. "This is the best news. We'll have a family."

"And be a family." She embraced him, and he tightened his arms around her.

As they held each other, Pei Ling's wrist comm beeped. She reluctantly pulled away from Zafer to answer it. It was Bai, and he sounded angry.

"Pei Ling, why didn't you come with us?" he demanded, his voice filled with frustration.

Pei Ling took a deep breath, seeming as though she was trying to keep calm. "Bai, I told you before that I can't just abandon Zafer. He's my mate, and I love him."

Bai scoffed on the other end of the line. "Love? You barely know him. He's an alien. He's not one of us."

Pei Ling scowled at her brother's words, and her tone was angry. "He's more than that, Bai. He's the father of my child. I can't just leave him."

There was a long pause on the other end of the line before Bai spoke again. "Fine, but you're making a mistake. You're choosing him over your family."

"I'm not choosing anyone over anyone, Bai. I love you and Mom and Dad and Mei. I just can't leave Zafer."

Bai sighed. "I hope you know what you're doing. We're leaving the planet without you."

She flinched, and he wanted to reach out and hold her again, to soothe her. "Bai, wait," she said, but he'd already ended the call.

Zafer put a hand on her shoulder, trying to convey his concern. "What happened?" he asked, though he'd heard at least the angry parts of the conversation when their voices had been sharper. He thought he'd gotten the gist of the conversation, but he didn't want to assume anything.

Pei Ling shook her head, tears streaming down her face. "Bai and my parents left the planet without me. He's angry with me for choosing you over my family."

He wrapped his arms around her, holding her closely. "I'm sorry. I didn't mean to cause a rift between you and your family."

She shook her head. "You didn't cause anything. This is all on me. I made the choice to stay with you, and I don't regret it. I just wish my family could understand."

He pulled her closer still, keeping his voice soothing. "We'll get through this together. We'll make a life for ourselves and our child, and if possible, we'll find a way to include your family too, if they relent." He didn't know how they'd manage that, but he'd try if it made her happy. He'd do anything to please his mate.

Pei Ling smiled weakly as her hand moved to rest on her stomach. "I want that. I want to stay with you for always."

Zafer kissed her forehead, his heart overflowing with love for her. "Then we'll be together for always."

They stayed like that for a while, holding each other close, before Pei Ling's wrist comm beeped again. It was a message from Mei. When he moved back to give her some privacy, she grasped his hand, so he stayed beside her.

Shamelessly, he read over her shoulder to see the message:

"Pei Ling, are you okay? Bai paid pirates to rescue me, but I didn't want to go. I'm happy with my mate. Beware if he approaches you."

Pei Ling smiled at the message, clearly relieved for her sister. She typed out a quick response.

"I'm okay, Mei. I'm safe. Bai and our parents left the planet without me. Stay with your mate. Don't let anyone force you to do something you don't want to do."

She hit send, looking content as she turned to Zafer, her eyes filled with determination. "I love you, Zafer. I meant that when I told Bai, and now I'm telling you directly."

His heart thumped relentlessly for a moment, and he drew in a deep breath so he could reply. His emotions threatened to overwhelm him. "And I love you, Pei Ling. You, and soon our baby, are the most important people in my life, and I'll always stand by you."

"I know you will, and I'll be standing right beside you too, no matter what."

He had no reason to doubt her words. With a groan, he bent his head to claim her mouth in a long kiss. They shared a tender kiss, sealing their love for each other. He was only vaguely aware of their surroundings until Quillin cleared his throat.

"That's not really letting her rest, and if you go on much longer, you'll cause a stir." The Med Chief sounded amused rather than outraged.

He pulled back and lifted Pei Ling into his arms. "I'll make sure she rests."

She pouted. "I want you."

"You'll have me, once you're recovered." With that, he swept her from Medbay and back to the docking port at the Embassy. If anyone stared, he didn't notice, because he had eyes only for his mate.

Epilogue

Pei Ling

PEI LING SAT NERVOUSLY in the passenger seat of their small spacecraft, holding their three-month-old daughter in her arms, with her eyes fixed on the swirling vortex ahead of them. This was the first jump point on their journey to Baxa, and the thought of leaving Earth for at least four years filled her with a sense of sadness and excitement all at once. She looked over at Zafer, who was piloting the ship with a focused expression on his face.

As they reached the jump point, Pei Ling took a deep breath and turned to Zafer. "I can't believe we're leaving Earth. It feels like this past year went so fast."

Zafer smiled at her, his hand reaching over to rest on her thigh. "I know, but we're starting a new chapter in our lives, and I couldn't be more excited to share it with you."

Pei Ling smiled back at him. She looked down at Lili, who was starting to fuss. "Speaking of sharing, I have some news."

His eyebrows rose. "What news?"

She took a deep breath, her heart racing. "I'm pregnant again," she said, her eyes locked on his.

Zafer's face lit with joy at the news. "Another baby?" He beamed, leaving no doubt he was thrilled. "That's amazing. I'm not surprised after your first heat following Lili's birth." He waggled his eyebrows.

She laughed as a sense of relief flooded through her at his reaction. "I was a little nervous about telling you. I didn't know if you were ready for another one yet."

Zafer chuckled, his hand reaching over to rub her belly. "Are you kidding? If I weren't, I would have used a barrier or gotten you a suppressant. I want a dozen," he said, his voice lighthearted, "But we can start with two for now."

Pei Ling rolled her eyes at the idea of a dozen offspring, though she was secretly amused. As they entered the jump point, and the ship lurched forward into the unknown, her thoughts were interrupted as her wrist comm beeped.

It was a message from her mother. She smiled as she read it, happy her family was safe and harbored no lasting ill-will toward her. They had settled on a planet far away from Earth, and while she didn't know the name or location, her parents and Bai regularly sent her updates and pictures of their new life.

Her mother's message was a picture of their new home, a small but cozy cottage surrounded by rolling hills and fields of vibrant green. *"We miss you and Mei, my dear, but we're happy here. Your father has taken up gardening, and Bai started a small business selling his artwork. We hope to see you soon, though Bai still insists we can't tell you where we are. I hope he'll come around someday or let us meet you somewhere. I want to cuddle my granddaughter before she's too big to hold."*

Pei Ling was content her family had found a new home and a new purpose. She typed out a quick response, including a picture of the sleeping Lili, along with sending love and well wishes to her parents and brother before turning her attention back to Zafer and their journey.

As they hit the second jump point, a wave of excitement washed over her. She looked down at their daughter, who was sleeping soundly in her arms, and then back at Zafer, who was grinning from ear to ear.

"Can you believe it?" he said, his voice filled with wonder. "We're starting a new life on a new planet with our family."

She smiled, feeling grateful they had gotten to this point. "I can't wait to see what the future holds for us. Who knows? Maybe we'll have a dozen children like you say you want."

He laughed, his eyes sparkling with love. "Maybe not a dozen, but I know we'll have a happy and full life together, my love." The words were full of the joy usually present in his voice these days.

It mirrored her own, and she settled back, content with life and pleased to have found her alphan mate. In retrospect, her previous fears seemed almost silly, and she was glad he'd taken the time to fetch his runaway proxy. He hadn't known she would be his mate, and she hadn't either, or she wouldn't have run, but he never had to worry about her running again. There was nowhere she wanted to be except by his side.

About Juno

JUNO WELLS GREW UP on Florida's Space Coast, watching the shuttles take off from Cape Canaveral. When she hit college, her childhood fantasies about space travel turned highly romantic. Now her mind reels with space adventures of fantastic alien lords in distant galaxies, and the earth women they love.

Wells' stories explore the complex, sensual relationships between inhabitants of different star systems. There are always happy endings just as there is always a new world to explore.

Have a comment? Make first contact with Juno at authorjunowells@gmail.com.

About Aurelia

AURELIA SKYE IS THE pen name *USA Today* Bestselling author Kit Tunstall uses when writing science fiction romance, paranormal romance, and paranormal women's fiction. It's simply a way to separate the myriad types of stories she writes so readers know what to expect with each "author."

Website[1]

---

1. http://www.kittunstall.com

Also by Aurelia Skye

Alien Baby Pact
Baby For The Grimlock General
Baby For The Palantir Chief
Baby For The Brundle Commander
Baby For The Alphan Captain
Baby For The Serp General
Alien Baby Pact Compilation
Baby For The Mosaic Med Chief
Baby For The Tark Commander

Alien Baby Pakt
Alien Baby Pakt Zusammenstellung

BioCircuit Nexus
Cyborgs' Origins
Cyborg's Tether
Cyborg's Love

Celestial Mates
Wrong Place, Right Mate
Destined For The Drakari Warlords

Cybernetic Hearts
Mated To The Cyborg General
Claimed By The Cyborg Commander
Fated For The Cyborg Officer
Meant For The Cyborg Captain
Baby For The Cyborg General
Cybernetic Hearts: Complete Series
Cœurs Cybernétiques: Série Complète

Dazon Agenda
Written In The Stars
Alien's Babies
Diplomatic Affairs
Moon Madness
Across The Stars
Emperor's Assassin Bride
Dazon Agenda: Complete Collection
Compilation de l'Agenda Dazon

Evershift Haven

Pumpkin Spice and Orc's Delight
Howls & Harvest
Winter Wishes & Elven Kisses
A Snowstorm & A Stonehorn
Valentine's With A Vampire
Shamrocks & Second Chances
Eggsactly The Right Gargoyle
Barbells, Broomsticks & A Baby

Evershift Haven Serie, Edizione Italiana
Pumpkin Spice & Orc's Delight
Howls & Harvest – Edizione Italiana

Future Fairytales
Hooked

Guerriers Blessés
Chassé
Inlassable
Marqué
Justice
Compilation Guerriers Blessés

Harrow Bay

Hell Gates & Hot Flashes
Nightmares & Night Sweats
Warlocks & Wrinkles
Love Spells & Liver Spots
Phantasms & Presbyopia
Vampires & Varicose Veins
Mermaids & Mood Swings
Séances & Sagging Skin
Necromancy & Knee Pains
Marids & Memory Loss
Devil Deals & Dizzy Spells
Happy Endings & New Beginnings
Harrow Bay, Volume 1
Hellhounds & Mistletoe
Harrow Bay, Volume 2
Harrow Bay, Volume 3
Harrow Bay Complete Series

Harrow Bay, Édition Française
Hell Gates & Hot Flashes

Harrow Bucht Serie
Höllentore & Hitzewallungen
Alpträume Und Nachtschweiß
Hexenmeister & Falten
Liebeszauber Und Leberflecken
Phantasmen Und Alterssichtigkeit

Vampire und Krampfadern
Meerjungfrauen Und Stimmungsschwankungen
Séancen Und Schlaffe Haut
Nekromantie Und Knieschmerzen
Marids und Gedächtnisverlust
Teufelsgeschäfte Und Schwindelzauber
Happy Ends Und Neuanfängen
Höllenhunde & Mistelzweige

Hell Virus
Catching Hell
Surviving Hell
Bleeding Hell
Raising Hell
Sharing Hell

Howls Romance
The Jaguar Alpha's Forbidden Lover
CEO Wolf Shifter's Surprise Twins

Northstar Shifters
Northstar Heir's Scarred Mate

Olympus Station

Station Commander's Surrogate
Alien Prince's Secret Baby
Security Agent's Alien Bartender
Olympus Station Compilation

Pacte des Bébés Aliens
Compilation du Pacte des Bébés Aliens

SpicyShorts
Music In My Heart
Kilted Tentacle Monster: A Search for True Love

Sweet Escapes
Hook & Wendy

The Haunting of Clara Gray
Ghostly Awakening
Ghostly Harmonies

Three Crones Inn
Vastly Inn-proved
Ghastly Intentions

Grave Inn-tervention
Ghostly Inn-heritance
Three Crones Inn Compilation

Three Crones Inn (Drei Kronen Gasthaus)
GHOSTLY INN-TENTIONS (GEISTERHAFTES ERBE)

True North
True North #1: Death & Deception
True North #2: Rescued & Revelations
True North #3: Fire & Ice
True North #4: Enemies & Lovers
True North #5: Truth & Tiranog
True North #6: Fight & Flight
True North #7: Love & Loss

Wounded Warriors
Relentless
Marked
Justice
Wounded Warriors Collection
Hunted

Standalone

Reluctant Companion
Princess By Mistake
Fire Lord's Assistant
True North
Dragon Laird's Witch
Alien General's Rebel Consort
Tempted By Demons
Enemy Combatant
Grotesquerie
Mistaken Bounty
Wahre Richtung
Power Surges & Amorous Urges
Taken By The Orc General
Compilación Pacto de Alienígena Descendencia

Also by Juno Wells

Alien Baby Pact
Baby For The Grimlock General
Baby For The Palantir Chief
Baby For The Brundle Commander
Baby For The Alphan Captain
Baby For The Serp General
Alien Baby Pact Compilation
Baby For The Mosaic Med Chief
Baby For The Tark Commander

Alien Baby Pakt
Alien Baby Pakt Zusammenstellung

BioCircuit Nexus
Cyborgs' Origins
Cyborg's Tether
Cyborg's Love

Dazon Agenda
Written In The Stars
Alien's Babies
Diplomatic Affairs
Moon Madness
Across The Stars
Emperor's Assassin Bride
Dazon Agenda: Complete Collection
Compilation de l'Agenda Dazon

Galactic Alphas
Alpha's Omega
Buying His Omega
Claiming His Omega
Galactic Alphas Compilation

Pacte des Bébés Aliens
Compilation du Pacte des Bébés Aliens

Standalone
Alien General's Rebel Consort
Compilación Pacto de Alienígena Descendencia

www.ingramcontent.com/pod-product-compliance
Lightning Source LLC
Chambersburg PA
CBHW052218150726
48002CB00003B/1167